Trolls
WORLD TOUR

A TROLL NEW WORLD

Adapted by Erin Rose Wage

we make books come alive®
Phoenix International Publications, Inc.
Chicago • London • New York • Hamburg • Mexico City • Sydney

N
E
S
W

POWER OF THE STRINGS
In the beginning, all Trolls worshipped a magical instrument with six special strings—each made from a strand of Troll hair. But then the Troll elders split up the strings among six different Troll tribes, in order to protect the power that the strings make when they're together.
Tour the different Troll tribes and find these unique vibrations:
techno string
funk string
pop string
rock string
classical string
country western string

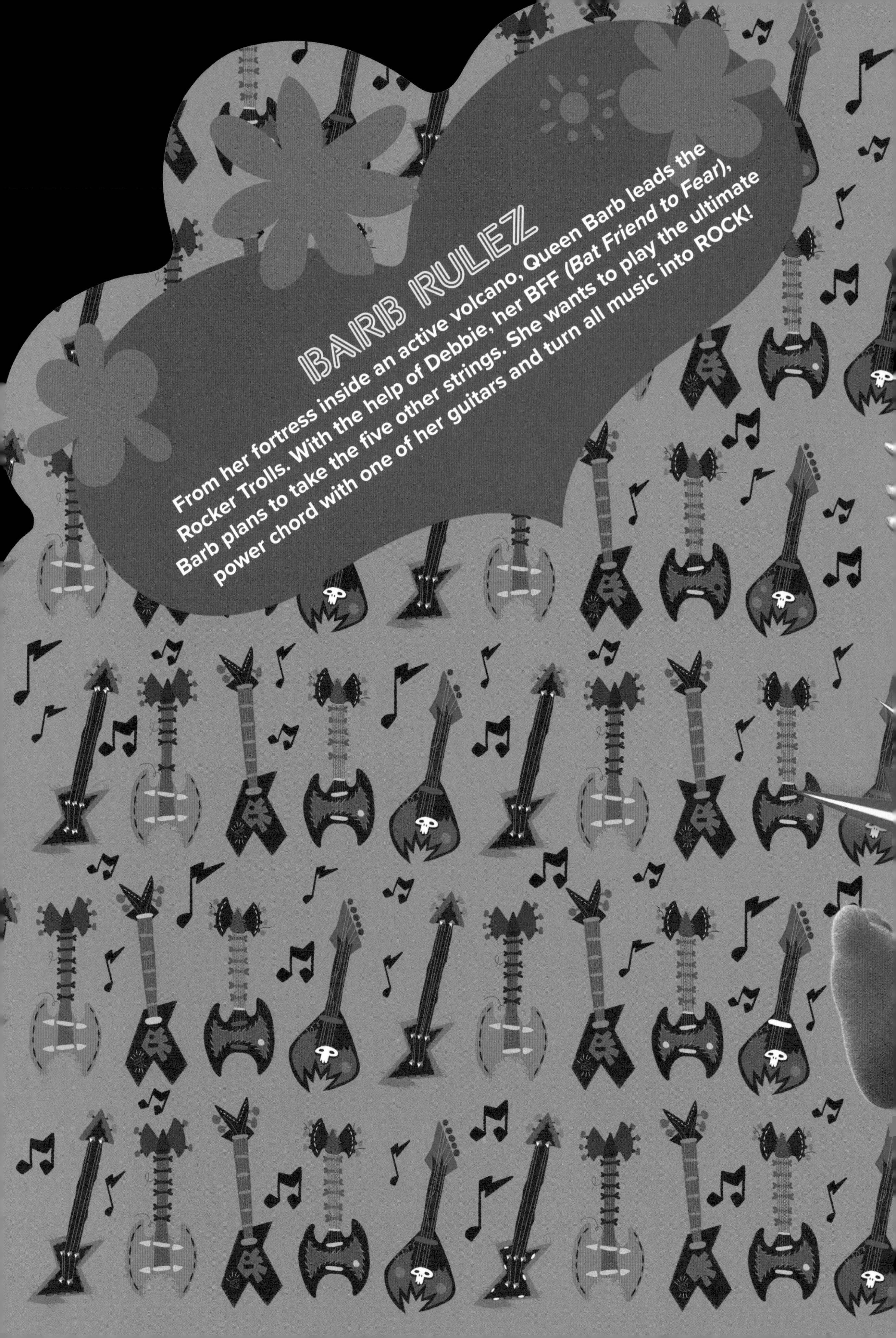

BARB RULEZ

From her fortress inside an active volcano, Queen Barb leads the Rocker Trolls. With the help of Debbie, her **BFF** *(Bat Friend to Fear)*, Barb plans to take the five other strings. She wants to play the ultimate power chord with one of her guitars and turn all music into **ROCK!**

QUEEN BARB
Shred through these gnarly guitars and find Barb's favorites:

RHYTHM AND RAINBOWS

Queen Poppy thinks music should make everyone happy. Pop beats make her the most upbeat, and she wants to share that with all of Trolls Kingdom! As she travels around the different villages, she leaves a trail of rainbows, glitter, and catchy pop rhythms.

Pump up the volume and count six of these rainbow roller skates and six pairs of these glittery glasses:

TROLL LOTTA LOVE

The Trolls of Trolls Village love to sing and dance and hug—especially to the infectious pop beats that their Queen Poppy shares on a daily basis. They fill their lives and their village with sunshine, rainbows, and glitter. So when they shake their hair, they positively SPARKLE!

Go door-to-door and find these
bedazzled little pod dwellers:

DROP THAT BEAT

Deep beneath the sea, Techno Troll mermaids swim through a digital fortress lit by LEDs. King Trollex, the leader of the Techno Trolls, rules over the Techno Reef, often from his glowing DJ booth. One of his most important royal duties is dropping the beat!

Swim through the pixels to find these creatures enjoying Trollex's DJ skills:

HERE COMES TREBLE

Conductor Wolfgang Amadeus Trollzart leads the Classical Trolls of Symphonyville. Life here is a symphony! Trollzart taps his baton and away they go. With a flourish to the left, the strings rise to a crescendo. A wave to the right, and Pennywhistle gives it her all.

Read through the sheet music
to find these notes:

COUNTRY BESTERN

The Trolls of Lonesome Flats embrace sadness through the power of Country Western music. But their love of sorrowful songs doesn't mean that they are sad sad. Their way of life just gives them an appreciation for a variety of feelings. And a variety of flannel, gingham, and hats!

Tune up your banjo and find these hair-accenting hats:

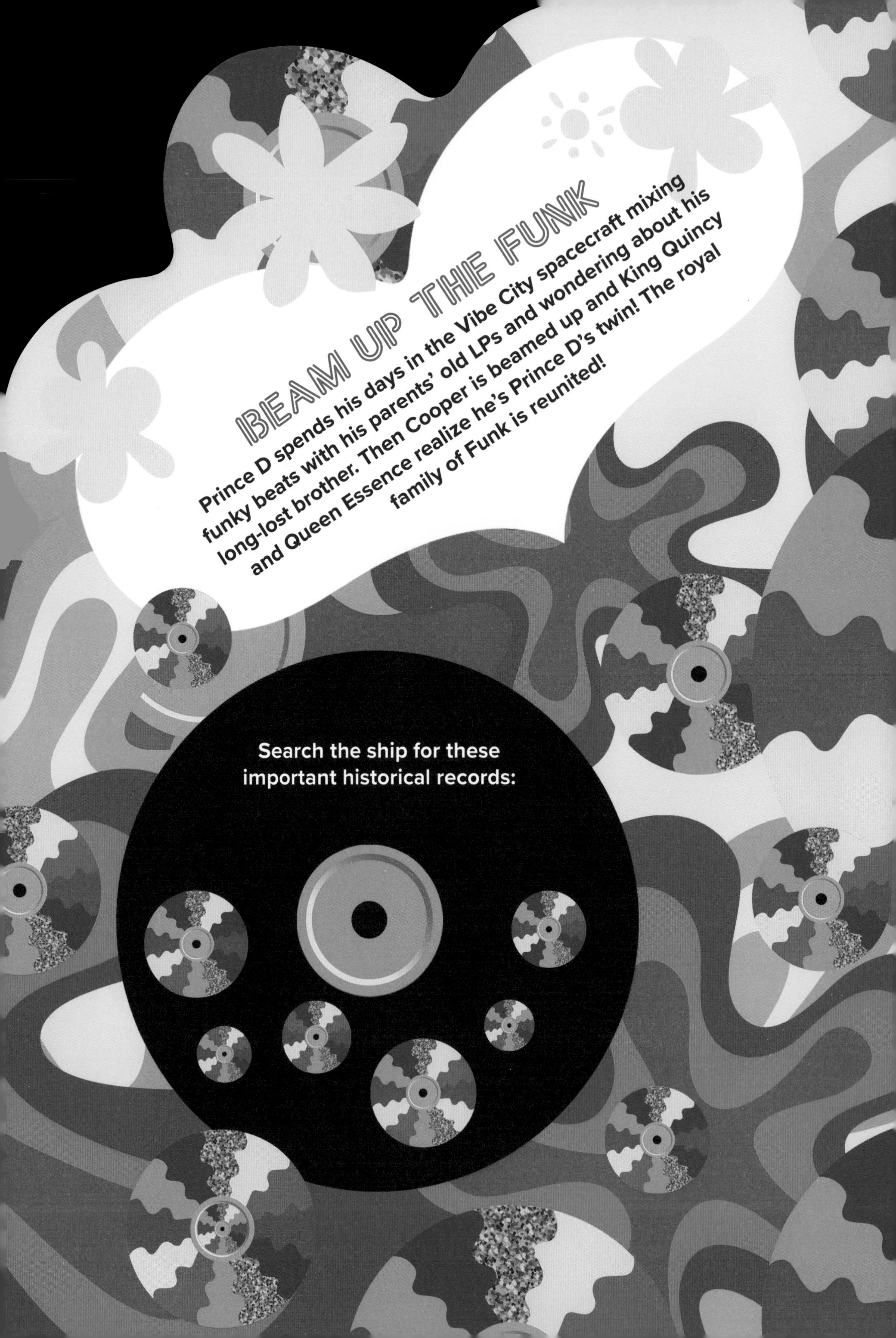

BEAM UP THE FUNK

Prince D spends his days in the Vibe City spacecraft mixing funky beats with his parents' old LPs and wondering about his long-lost brother. Then Cooper is beamed up and King Quincy and Queen Essence realize he's Prince D's twin! The royal family of Funk is reunited!

Search the ship for these important historical records:

RESPECT THE ROCK

Volcano Rock City is home to the Rocker Trolls. Decked out in denim and patches, these Trolls live on the edge—which is extra-dangerous since the volcano is active. But banging their heads to Queen Barb's bone-rattling guitar riffs is worth the heat.

Mosh through the volcano
and find these wicked skulls:

MUSIC IS LIFE
The separate tribes that make up all of Trolls Kingdom are very different. But while they each march to a *different* beat, they all live for the *same* thing—music! They sing songs that celebrate their lives and culture, and express their unique Trollness.

Pick out these different instruments that each have a distinct voice:

TROLLS WORLD TOUR!
Why listen to one kind of music, or dance with one kind of Troll?
The Troll villages are putting on concerts, so get your tickets
before they sell out! You can rock out, get funky, shed a tear,
drop a beat, tap a baton, and DANCE!
Stop by the merch table
and find these fists before
they snag your swag:

Customer Service: 1-877-277-9441 or customerservice@pikidsmedia.com

Published by Phoenix International Publications, Inc.
8501 West Higgins Road
Chicago, Illinois 60631

59 Gloucester Place
London W1U 8JJ

www.pikidsmedia.com

8 7 6 5 4 3 2 1

ISBN: 978-1-5037-5232-0